Based on the TV series *Rugrats*® created by Arlene Klasky, Gabor Csupo, and
Paul Germain as seen on BBC tv

An imprint of Simon & Schuster UK Ltd
Africa House, 64-78 Kingsway, London WC2B 6AH

A CIP catalogue record for this book is available
from the British Library

ISBN 0671 773208

Printed in Hong Kong by Midas Printing Ltd.

1 3 5 7 9 10 8 6 4 2

The Bestest Mum

Adapted by Susan Hood
from the script by Jon Cooksey, Ali Marie Matheson,
David Weiss, and J. David Stern

Illustrated by Ed Resto

POCKET
BOOKS

"Hey!" said Angelica, as she walked in to find the Rugrats playing with her bowl of macaroni. "What are you babies doing? I'm using that to make a present for my mum!"

The babies stared at her.

"Why are you giving your mum a present?" asked Phil.

"You babies are so dumb," said Angelica. "I can't believe you lived to be one. Today is Mother's Day—the day everybody gives their mum presents! Now get out of here and let me work!"

"We don't got a present for our mum," said Lil.

"I bet if we look around we can find things our mums will like," said Tommy. They decided to look where they had always found the best presents for each other—in the couch!

Tommy found a hairy biscuit. Lil found Grandpa Lou's glasses.

Just then the doorbell rang. It was Chuckie and his dad.

"Hi, Chuckie," said Tommy. "Want to help us find Mother's Day presents?"

"Okay, but who would I give a present to?" asked Chuckie.

"Oh, yeah," said Lil. "You don't got a mum, do you, Chuckie?"

"Nope," said Chuckie.

"How come?" asked Phil.

"I don't know," said Chuckie. "I just don't got one."

The babies kept looking for presents. As they searched the garden, Lil remembered the first present she and Phil had given their mum. "'Member, Phil?" she asked. "It was back when we use'ta be hungry all the time and Mum fed us the old way."

Phil remembered. He had tickled Lil's feet, which made her giggle, and then he giggled.

"It was our first laugh," said Lil. "Mum says that was the best present we ever gave her."

"Don't you remember *ever* havin' a mum?" Lil asked Chuckie.

"No," said Chuckie. "Sometimes I dream about havin' a mum, though. It's always the same dream too. We're always outside. There's lotsa grass and flowers. I think she likes the flowers. And there's a butterfly—and I'm not even afraid of it."

The babies sighed. They had to find a mum for Chuckie!

Finding a mum wasn't easy, but Tommy had an idea. His mother had a dress dummy. And when she hung clothes on it, it sort of looked like a mum.

But when Chuckie hugged the dummy, it felt cold and bumpy—not what he thought a mum should be. "At least I got a hug," said Chuckie, "sort of."

"I think we should find Chuckie a mummy who can give kisses, too," said Lil.

Tommy knew someone who gave great kisses.

"Yuck!" said Chuckie as Spike slobbered all over his glasses.

Everyone decided that mums weren't supposed to be dogs. They were supposed to be people. Maybe Lil could be a mum!

Lil tried hard to be a good mummy.
She cleaned her baby's messy face.

Then she looked under the fridge.
Lil found an old baby bottle and brushed
the ants off. Most of them, anyway.

Finally, she gave the bottle to her baby.

"Come on widdew Chuckums," said Lil, as she tried to pick up her runaway baby. "Time to burp the snoogy-oogums!"

"Stop it, Lil," said Chuckie. "I don't need to burp! Besides, you're a worser mum than Spike. You spit on my face. You give me ant milk."

"You're just cranky 'cause you need a nap," said Lil.

"Whoaaaa!" screamed Chuckie as they toppled backwards and a wastepaper basket landed on Chuckie's head.

Just then Angelica walked by, grumbling under her breath. "Why do I have to spend the whole day working just because it's Mother's Day?" she said. Then she noticed Chuckie.

"What's his problem?" she asked.

"Chuckie's sad 'cause he don't got a mum," Phil said.

"Hmm," Angelica thought. "If I was a mum, then somebody would have to do everything for me."

"I s'pose I could be his mum," Angelica said sweetly. "But you know I'm very busy with my macaroadie head."

"I could help you!" said Chuckie.

"Well . . . okay, son," said Angelica, with a sly smile.

A little later the babies went to check on Chuckie. They felt sorry for him, having Angelica for a mum.

"Hey," yelled Angelica. "Blaine is busy."

"Who's Blaine?" asked Tommy.

"He is. Chuckie is a stupid name. Blaine is a TV name. And since Blaine is busy, you babies have to run along. Right, Blaine?"

"Right, Angelica-mum," said Chuckie, sheepishly. "Sorry, guys, I gotta get back to work."

When the noodle head was done, Angelica wanted a flower to put on top. She led Chuckie outside and pointed to the most perfect flower. "I want that one," she said.

"But there's a mumblebee on it!" said Chuckie, trembling with fright.

"Oh, never mind, Blaine," said Angelica, sobbing fake tears. "I'll just tell my mum there's no present for her this year! Boo hoo hoo."

"Don't cry, Angelica-mum," said Chuckie bravely. "I'll get it."

Chuckie grabbed the flower. "AHHH! BEE! AHHHH!" he screamed as he ran away from the buzzing bee.

"Uh, Angelica-mum," said Chuckie. "I got your flower."

"All I wanted was one little flower!" screamed Angelica. "And you gaved me this! After all I've done for you."

Chuckie felt awful. "I'm sorry, Angelica-mum," he said, backing away.

Suddenly there was a crash! Chuckie had walked into the macaroni head, and now it lay in a big noodle-y mess on the floor.

Angelica was furious. "That does it!" she yelled. "You're all in time out!"

Angelica marched the babies into the hall cupboard and stormed off.
"Chuckie," she yelled, "you can forget about havin' a mum. Ever!"

Chuckie hung his head. "I don't deserve to have a mum," he said sadly.

"Sure you do, Chuckie," said Phil, "but you deserve a good mum. Not like Angelica. A mum who can kiss cuts and make them better."

"An' help you do things you never thought you could do," said Lil. "Like walk."

"A mum who'd love you and your flower," added Tommy. "Even if it is just a green stick with a thing on it."

"Hey," said Chuckie. "I just thought of somethin'. I sorta have a mum like that . . ."

"My dad!" said Chuckie.
"He's the bestest mum ever!"

Now that the babies had found Chuckie a mum, they got busy looking for presents in the cupboard. Tommy found a toilet plunger. Lil found a shoebox. Inside the box was a trowel, a book full of pressed flowers, and a photograph.

"Hey!" said Chuckie, as he stared at the picture. "It's the lady I told you about! From my dreams!"

DIARY

Soon the babies heard grown-up voices in the front hall. Their mums and dads were home! The kids tumbled out of the cupboard holding their gifts. The parents laughed and smiled, except for Chuckie's dad. He seemed upset.

"Chaz," whispered Didi, "I know I was keeping these for you, but I think it's time you shared these things with Chuckie."

"I'm just afraid he'll miss her," said Chaz.

"Then you can miss her together," she said, squeezing his arm.

Chaz took Chuckie home and pulled him onto his lap with the shoebox that had been in the cupboard.

"Chuckie," said Chaz, as he held up the photograph. "This is your mummy. This is her trowel and over there is her garden. She used to love to come out here and play with you."

Then Chaz pulled out a diary and said, "Your mum started keeping this diary when she was in the hospital. The last thing she wrote in it was a poem. *For you.*"

My Sweet Little Chuckie,
Though I must leave you behind me,
This poem will tell you
Where you always can find me.

When a gentle wind blows,
That's my hand on your face.
When the tree gives you shade,
That's my sheltering embrace.

When the sun gives you freckles,
That's me tickling my boy.
When the rain wets your hair,
Those are my tears of joy.

When the long grass enfolds you,
That's me holding you tight.
When the whippoorwill sings,
That's me whispering... night-night....

"Gee," said Chuckie. "I do have a mum. She's right here in the flowers—"

"And in the clouds," said Chaz, tossing his son up in the air, "and in the grass . . . and in the sun—"

"And in the wind . . ." laughed Chuckie, as a butterfly tickled his nose.